# One Duck Stuck

## Phyllis Root illustrated by Jane Chapman

**WALKER BOOKS**
AND SUBSIDIARIES
LONDON · BOSTON · SYDNEY

**D**own by the marsh,
by the sleepy,
slimy marsh,

**1**

one duck
gets stuck in the muck,
down by the
deep green marsh.

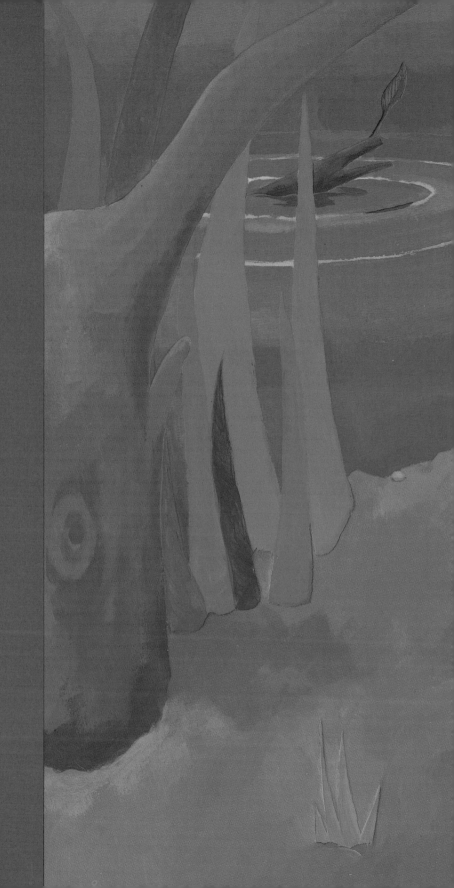

Help!
Help!

Who
can
help?

# We can! We can!

2

Two fish,
tails going swish,
swim to the duck.

## Splish, splish.

No luck.
The duck stays stuck
deep in the muck
down by the
squishy, fishy marsh.

Help!
Help!

Who
can
help?

# We can! We can!

3

Three moose
munching on spruce
plod to the duck.

## Clomp, clomp.

No luck.
The duck stays stuck
deep in the muck
down by the
swampy, chompy marsh.

Help!
Help!

Who
can
help?

# We can! We can!

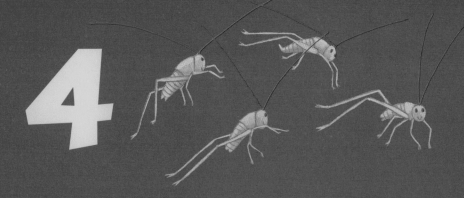

**4**

Four crickets
chirping in the thickets
leap to the duck.

## Pleep, pleep.

No luck.
The duck stays stuck
deep in the muck
down by the
pricky, sticky marsh.

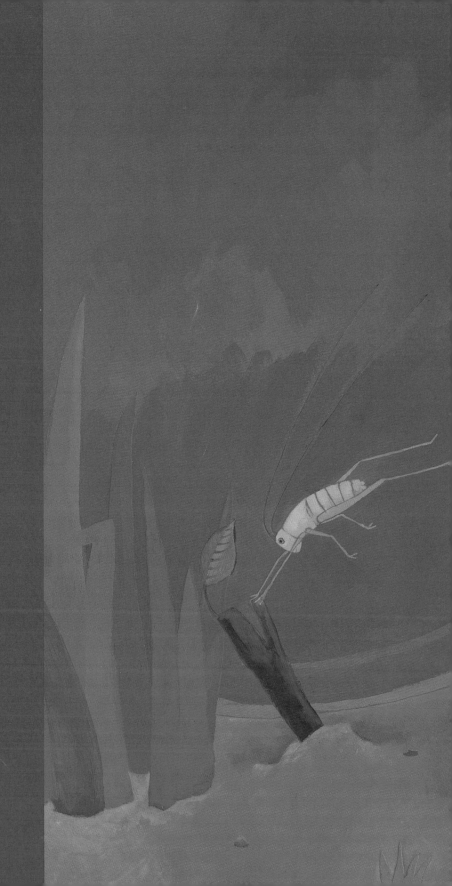

Help!
Help!

Who
can
help?

# We can! We can!

**5**

Five frogs
hopping on logs
jump to the duck.

## Plop, plop.

No luck.
The duck stays stuck
deep in the muck
down by the
creaky, croaky marsh.

# We can! We can!

6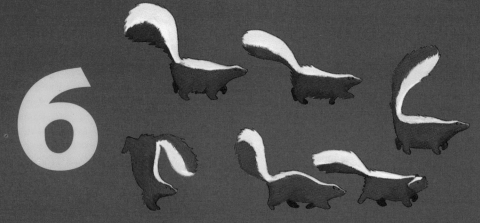

Six skunks
climbing over trunks
crawl to the duck.

## Plunk, plunk.

No luck.
The duck stays stuck
deep in the muck
down by the
soggy, loggy marsh.

Help!
Help!

Who
can
help?

# We can! We can!

**7**

Seven snails
making slippery trails
slide to the duck.

## Sloosh, sloosh.

No luck.
The duck stays stuck
deep in the muck
down by the
slippy, sloppy marsh.

Help! Help!

Who can help?

# We can! We can!

**8**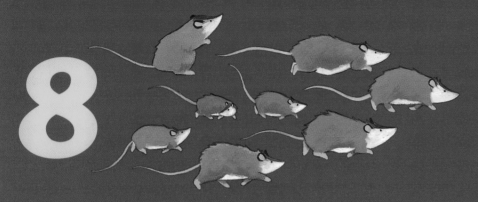

Eight possums
nibbling on blossoms
crawl to the duck.

## Slosh, slosh.

No luck.
The duck stays stuck
deep in the muck
down by the
reedy, weedy marsh.

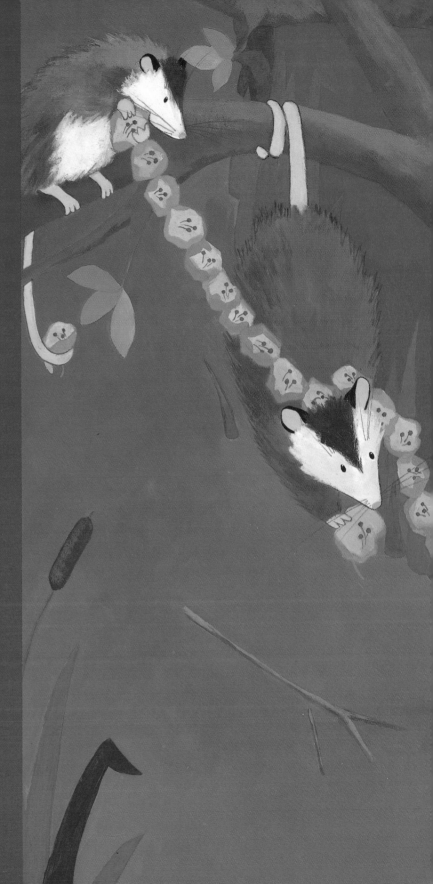

Help!
Help!

Who
can
help?

# We can! We can!

**9**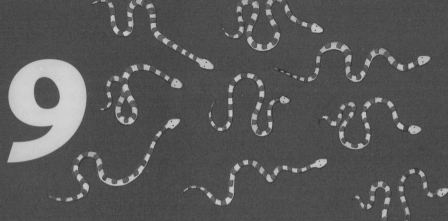

Nine snakes
leaving little wakes
slither to the duck.

## Slink, slink.

No luck.
The duck stays stuck
deep in the muck
down by the
messy, mossy marsh.

Help!
Help!

Who
can
help?

# We can! We can!

**10**

Ten dragonflies
zooming through the skies
whirr to the duck.

## Zing, zing.

No luck.
The duck stays stuck
deep in the muck
down by the
muggy, buggy marsh.

Help!
Help!

Who
can
help?

We can!

We can!

plunk

sloosh

slosh

slink

zing

They **all** help the duck who got stuck in the muck.

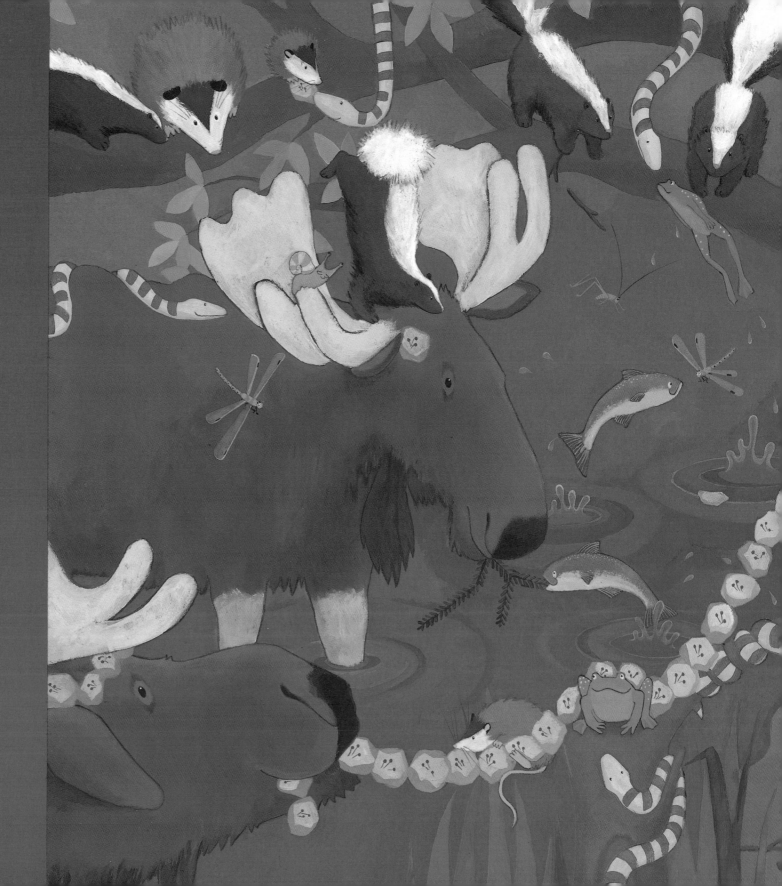

Spluck!

**"Thanks!"**
said the duck
who got out
of the muck

down

by the

deep

green

marsh.